Doin' It

Ayshia Monroe

SADDLEBACK
EDUCATIONAL PUBLISHING

2/13
PA

SADDLEBACK
EDUCATIONAL PUBLISHING
www.sdlback.com

ISBN-13: 978-1-61651-669-7
ISBN-10: 1-61651-669-0
eBook: 978-1-61247-641-4

Printed in Guangzhou, China
0712/CA21201001

16 15 14 13 12   1 2 3 4 5

Kiki Butler sat on the bottom bleacher of what passed for the South Central High School football stadium—really two sets of risers on either side of a weed-strewn field. Her classmates were sprawled out on seats behind her. Most had eyes glued to their cell phones. Nobody dared text—that was against school rules—but there was no rule against clock watching.

Kiki didn't have her cell out, since she was actually paying attention to her English teacher, Ms. Okoro. That didn't mean she couldn't sneak a peek at the phone of the person sitting next to her, though.

"Ten thirty," Kiki thought. "Twelve more minutes here. Then one more class. And then no more school. What a year. What an effing year."

Kiki knew her classmates were craving the final bell that signaled sleeping in and partying off the hook. She herself wasn't much of a party girl—she much preferred the basketball court to doing shots and smoking herb—but she had a good summer ahead. There'd be plenty of time to hang with her boyfriend, Sean King. She'd be working at the day-care at Northeast Towers, the two-building apartment project where she lived with her older-by-two-minutes twin sister, Sherise, her mom, and her stepdad.

Since the weather was so great—sunny, calm, temp in the seventies—Ms. Okoro (everyone just called her Ms. O) had brought the eleventh grade English class outside. Ms. O had been born and raised in Nigeria and wore a festive orange dress and a ton of bracelets in honor of this last day of school. She often spoke of how teachers in Africa were treated with reverence and how kids went to school dressed nicely.

"South Central High sure ain't Africa," Kiki thought. "Even if school be savage!"

Kiki took in her own cutoff jeans, Chicago Bulls jersey, and basketball kicks. Pretty tall at five foot eight, her hair was back in her usual braids after an experimental new 'do for prom. Her classmates were as casual as she was, except for Tia Ramirez, who sat a few rows back. Tia had come to the hood from Mexico a year or so ago. She wore a beige pants suit with her dark hair in a thick bun and glasses perched on her head.

Tia always dress like she goin' to court to testify.

"Christopher Okigbo was not just a poet," Ms. Okoro spoke without notes. "He was a poet, and he was a revolutionary. He died in a rebellion against the Nigerian government in the late 1960s. Listen!"

I have fed out of the drum!
I have drunk out of the cymbal!
I have entered your bridal chamber;
    and lo,
I am the sole witness to my
    homecoming!

"Okigbo wrote that in a poem called 'Distances,'" Ms. O said. "And the homecoming he is talking about is not high school homecoming. But I'll spare you analysis and let you enjoy the words." She stepped toward the bleachers, made a big show of glancing at someone's phone—kids laughed at that—and then smiled.

"Just another hour and you're out for the summer. That gives me time to be a witness to something important. Kiki, Tia, and Nishell Saunders, could you join me?"

Kiki was taken by surprise. She looked back at Tia and then at Nishell. Nishell was super-curvy. She wore jeans and a black leotard shirt and had her camera around her neck. She'd been head photographer at yearbook club, and Tia had been manager. Kiki had worked on the yearbook too.

She and the girls approached Ms. O, and Kiki gazed out at their classmates. Jackson Beauford—Nishell's boyfriend—was elbowing the kid next to him. Behind Jackson was Carlos Howard, Sherise's boyfriend. He looked ready to fall asleep.

"See these three students?" Ms. O asked. "I learned in Africa that school is not here to teach you. It is here to give you the opportunity to learn! 'I have fed out of the drum; I have drunk out of the cymbal.' Okigbo is saying that in order to live and learn, one must act. Kiki, Tia, and Nishell worked hard on the yearbook. They lived and learned. They acted. They deserve recognition."

Ms. O spread her arms wide. "Recognize!" she ordered.

To Kiki's shock, her classmates applauded. Kiki saw Nishell grin wildly. Tia was nodding slightly, as if she felt she deserved the props. Kiki herself felt great.

No one ever recognizes me.

A few moments later, though, Kiki wasn't feeling so good.

As the applause died, someone stepped out around the bleachers. It was

Miss Prince, the secretary in the guidance office. She was so old Kiki figured she'd worked there since Abraham Lincoln was president. She reported to Mr. Crandall, the head guidance counselor, whom everyone hated.

For good reason. Crandall be an ass.

Miss Prince cleared her throat loudly and then spoke. "Ms. Okoro, pardon the interruption. Mr. Crandall wants to see two of your students immediately. Shemeka—Kiki—Butler and Tia Ramirez, please follow me."

It was never good to be called into Crandall's office. It could mean only one thing. You were in trouble.

"Whatchu think this be about?" she asked Tia.

The girl from Mexico shrugged. "I have no idea."

Kiki noticed that Tia's Mexican accent was practically gone. She sounded almost like she'd spoken English her whole life.

"He gonna mess us up for something," Kiki predicted glumly.

As they waited for Crandall, Kiki stared at the bad artwork on his walls. Crandall loved bird paintings.

What kind of bird would Crandall be? A pigeon? A wren? Nah. Prolly a vulture.

The door opened. Crandall entered. He was close to retirement age, with graying hair and rheumy blue eyes. He also had the worst taste in clothes of any human on the planet. Today he wore a black suit with an orange tie.

Crandall wasn't alone. With him was the school principal, Mr. Olson, also in a bad suit and tie. Olson had done a poor job at school after school before the board of education dumped him at SCHS. He mostly hid in his office.

He don't dress no better than Crandall. I ain't never talked to him. Well, I'm gonna hear from him now.

The tension was too great for Kiki to shut up any longer.

"What'd we do?" Kiki blurted.

The two adults were taken aback, and then laughed.

"I don't know why you assume it's bad news," Mr. Olson said.

"In *this* office?" Kiki scowled. "It's always bad news."

She looked at Tia. The other girl sat impassively, hands folded, legs crossed.

Mr. Olson smiled. He had bad teeth. "Not today. Why don't you explain, Mr. Crandall?"

"Gladly," Crandall's voice was friendly. Kiki figured he was probably trying to impress his boss.

"Kiki, Tia, I've seen your final grades. You two are tied for the highest grade point average in the junior class. Congratulations to you both."

Tia responded first. "Thank you, sir!"

"Thank you," Kiki echoed, shocked. She had done well. But tied for first in the class? This was incredible.

Crandall wasn't done, though.

"At this rate, it's a safe bet that one of you will be valedictorian next June. After that will surely be college."

"If we can afford it!" Kiki responded.

Kiki knew she was speaking for Tia as well as herself. She and Tia weren't friends. Tia was just too intense; all she wanted was to get ahead. If that meant someone had to be stepped on to get there, that was life. Still, Kiki admired her. Tia was a stranger in this strange land called America, and her family didn't have any more money than Kiki's family. But Tia worked her butt off.

"You don't have to worry about the cost of college, girls. Considering your … er … economic situations, there will be scholarships," the principal promised.

"College is more than tuition," Tia reminded. "There are fees, books, food—"

"That may not cost you a cent," Crandall declared.

Kiki frowned. "What do you mean?"

"For Pete's sake, Charlie. Just tell them!" the principal ordered, calling Crandall by a first name Kiki didn't even know he had.

"Okay." Crandall faced the girls. "Here's the thing. Big Boss Dawkins—the businessman from our neighborhood who paid for your prom—has created a new scholarship, the Big Boss Scholarship. It goes to the class valedictorian and covers everything a regular scholarship won't, including living expenses and spending money. If you end next year with identical grade point averages, you'll share it."

Kiki sank into her seat, her hand floating to her open mouth.

Holy holy omigod.

It wasn't that college hadn't been talked about in Kiki's apartment, because it had. Her stepfather had a master's in social work, and her mother an associate's degree. It was understood, though, that even with scholarships, the best she and her sister could hope for would be the state university.

Tia recovered first. She dead-eyed Crandall. "If that's true, the winner can go to any school that takes her. Harvard, Yale, USC—"

"That's correct," Mr. Olson agreed. "The scholarship even covers airfare."

Stunned, Kiki's hand was still by her mouth. She was too shocked to move.

"Everything must now be thought of in terms of applying to the schools of your choice and what will look best on your applications," Crandall counseled. "You girls have been handed a remarkable opportunity. I suggest you take it."

Kiki was finally ready to say something. She turned to Tia, whom she didn't like very much. "Congratulations, Tia. I hope we both win."

CHAPTER

2

Kiki sat at a small round table with Marnyke Cooper—her best friend from yearbook club—and Sean, not far from a dingy stage. On that stage was a scruffy but handsome white guy. He wore a black T-shirt, jeans, and bright purple basketball shoes. He had piercing green eyes, and an acoustic guitar was slung around his neck. After his band finished a set of punk rock that had given Kiki a headache, the boy was singing the final verse of a solo number.

Billie Joe sang about a fork that's
   in the road
One path not taken, another leads
   to our abode
We do our best to navigate this life
We dodge the grief, the anger, and
   the strife
My heart is faithful, my soul is
   always true
I just want to hold onto you

As the song ended, Kiki and Sean applauded politely. The rest of the crowd, though, went wild. So did Marnyke.

"Can you believe I met him in the hotel lobby at prom?" she gushed. "He so talented. Gabe be the bomb!"

Kiki exchanged a smile with Sean. Marnyke was so out the frame for the guy it wasn't even funny.

It was Friday night. Marnyke had talked Kiki and Sean into coming to this little club called Quadrangle to hear Gabe and his band. The place was near the industrial waterfront, a long way from Kiki's hood. It had graffiti-covered walls and waitresses with piercings in places that should never be pierced. That the crowd was mostly white high school kids posing and slumming was obvious from the moment she and Sean had pulled into the parking lot in Sean's rebuilt Ford Taurus.

'Cause the lot's full of BMWs and Lexuses.

Well, Gabe be from fancyville Majestic Oaks. These kids be his friends. What do you expect?

Kiki had dressed in jeans and a denim shirt. Sean, who was a skinny six foot one with kind eyes and an even kinder smile, had on baggy shorts and a blue shirt with white starbursts.

Marnyke had gone full-on sex bomb. She wore a skintight gray dress that barely covered her butt. If she was wearing a bra, Kiki couldn't tell. Her plump lips glistened with red lipstick. Her button nose was perfectly powdered.

Marnyke was a girl who'd flirt with anything that moved and appeared male. Tonight, though, Kiki saw she had eyes for just one man: Gabe.

"He comin' over here," Marnyke promised. "We can tell him he be the bomb."

Sean leaned toward Kiki. "You like the music?"

"His band? No way. Solo? He okay." Kiki's usual tastes ran to Beyoncé and Kanye, not rich, white emo-boys either banging guitars or crooning about rich, white emo-boy problems.

"He sounds like something my dentist would play," Sean murmured.

Kiki grinned. "You need to find you a new dentist."

"I need to get the deejay to play us some Tone Def."

"Hey, I heard that!" Marnyke cut in. "You just tight in your taste."

"Marnyke, I think the only thing you want to be tight with is that white boy," Kiki fired back.

"Hey, hey." Gabe slid into an empty chair. The club was emptier now as kids went outside to smoke whatever.

"Hey, baby." Marnyke snuggled up next to him.

"What'd you think?" Gabe asked her.

"I loved it!" Marnyke announced. She focused on Sean and Kiki. "Didn't you love it?"

When polite Kiki and Sean were slow to respond, Gabe easily filled the silence. "If it's not your thing, it's not your thing. Don't feel like you gotta stay all night."

"Thanks, man," Sean told him.

"Never apologize for your musical taste," Gabe went on. "I like Tone Def. I don't like Shing02. I love Yung Joc. I don't like Kid Cudi. I still think Gang Starr was genius. But nobody has to like everything. That's why they call it art."

"I guess not," Kiki said, impressed. Gabe obviously knew his hip-hop. That counted for something.

"We glad you came," Marnyke told Kiki. "Gabe and me got a surprise for you."

Surprise? What surprise?

Marnyke answered Kiki's unspoken question by reaching under the table and finding a bag that held a bottle of French champagne and four plastic glasses. Gabe expertly popped the cork, poured for everyone, and handed glasses around.

"Awww. I think I know what this for," Kiki thought. "Unless they gettin' married!"

Marnyke raised her full glass for a toast. "To the best student at South Central High School, who gonna win the Big Boss Scholarship, and who gonna be my bestie forever. Here's to Kiki!"

"Hear, hear!" Gabe added.

Kiki looked at Sean; he seemed delighted by the impromptu celebration. The four of them touched glasses and drank.

Then Gabe put the bottle in a brown paper sack and gave it to Sean. "The river's four blocks away, dude. Go for a walk with your brilliant girlfriend. Enjoy."

"Nah." Sean waved him off. "We gonna hang with—"

"Go," Gabe commanded. "Or I'm gonna get up there, sing the theme from *Barney*, and dedicate it to you."

Kiki cracked up. Sean did too. Marnyke wrapped herself around Gabe's left side.

"You got it goin' on, man," Sean told Gabe.

"I love you, Marnyke," Kiki told her friend.

Just before they were out the door, Kiki turned to wave at Marnyke and Gabe. They didn't wave back ... because they were latched in one hell of a lip lock.

"You want more?" Sean asked. He wiped his lips with the back of his wrist and offered the champagne to Kiki. "I'm not much of a drinker."

Kiki shook her head. "Me neither. How much is left?"

"Enough not to throw it away."

"Leave it for the street people," Kiki instructed. "They'll think they died and went to heaven."

It was twenty minutes later. Kiki and Sean had walked the four blocks to the riverfront where a narrow strip of park divided the factories from the water. There wasn't much boat traffic at this hour, and there weren't many people. With Sean, though, Kiki felt totally safe.

Sean put the paper-wrapped bottle on the ground where some patrolling wino would surely find it. "I think I'm the one who died and went to heaven."

"Whatchu mean?"

Sean looked serious. "Here I be wit' the smartest girl in the school. And the tenda-ist too. If that ain't heaven, I don't know what is."

Kiki felt herself flush. She knew she was smart. But even after the makeover she'd gotten for prom a couple of weeks back, she didn't feel very tender.

"Whatchu gonna do with all them smarts, Kiki?" Sean asked. "Be a doctor? Be a lawyer? Be president?"

"I'm gonna start by gettin' into a good school and splittin' that scholarship with

Tia," Kiki told him. She leaned against the iron railing that separated the path from the river and inhaled the humid evening air. "What about you?"

Sean joined her. "You know what I like, Kiki. I like basketball, and I like fixing cars. I'm gonna open me a combo gym and repair shop."

He'd said it so deadpan that Kiki bought it.

Then Sean laughed. "Just the repair shop, anyway. Unless I get a chance to race Maseratis."

"Hey! Maybe you will!" Kiki encouraged, elbowing him gently.

"Nah. Ain't gonna happen. I'm workin' at Mendoza's Garage this summer. Best I can hope for is a shop of my own. That ain't a bad life, I guess."

For a few moments, the two of them watched the river current dance in the moonlight.

—

"I don't get it, Kiki," Sean said suddenly.

"Get what?"

"Get why you be so into me. I ain't never gotten better than a C in my life."

Sean's voice was so sad that Kiki put a hand on his cheek and turned his face toward hers.

"You a good person, Sean," she said honestly. "You ain't a playa. You don't drink much. You don't smoke much. You fine, and you real." Then she grinned slyly. "An' you got a money fade-away jump shot. What girl wouldn't want to be wit' you?"

The answer seemed to satisfy him.

He kissed her.

She kissed him back.

CHAPTER

3

"Welcome to the Fat Man," boomed the elderly waitress, whose name was Geraldine and who talked a mile a minute. "Best damn soul food north of the Big D and east of Oakland."

The Fat Man was a local legend. Located at the east end of Twenty-Third Street near the cross with King Memorial Drive, the soul food palace had seen a lot of history. It had been a Black Panthers hangout in the 1960s, and there were pictures on the walls of the founder with civil rights leaders. When a politician campaigned in town, there was an unwritten law that he or she had to stop in at the Fat Man for chitlins and okra.

Tyson and LaTreece liked to take Kiki and Sherise there for breakfast on special occasions. The day after Kiki found out she was up for the scholarship definitely qualified as a special occasion.

"We got fresh biscuits." Geraldine rattled on, "We got eggs that the Fat Man done plucked from the henhouse this morning. We got flapjacks. We got ham so fresh that yesterday it was squealin'. We got juice I squeezed myself and coffee brewin'. Now, Tyson Nelson, what can we get you and your fine-lookin' brood this morning?"

"Two orders scrambled, two orders sunny-side up, biscuits and gravy, a plate of grits, side of sausage, side of bacon, toast, coffee, four coffee cakes, and don't get on my case 'bout my cholesterol, Geraldine," Tyson told her.

Geraldine didn't write any of their order down. She had a crazy good memory. "Don't have to mention it, Tyson. You just did."

"Busted!" Kiki exclaimed over the restaurant din.

The Fat Man was always jammed on weekend mornings. Kiki had come in the jeans and T-shirt that she'd been told to wear for her first day at the day-care center. She was starting her summer job at noon. Mrs. Phillips, who ran the day-care, had said that the first few days would be a probationary period to assess whether Kiki could do the job.

Kiki had no doubt that she could handle it. How tough could taking care of little kids be?

Geraldine took off and then reappeared a millisecond later with juice, coffee, and the coffee cake. Tyson helped pass it around.

"I want to remind everyone why we're here." He gazed with love at Kiki. "You're the reason, Kiki. I couldn't be any prouder of you if you were my own flesh and blood."

Before an embarrassed Kiki could say thank you, her mom gushed too. "You know all I ever did was two years of college. To think that my baby's going to Spellman—"

"Hold on!" Kiki protested. "I never said that!"

"But you could," LaTreece emphasized. "Or Stanford. Or even—"

"Um, excuse me?"

Kiki looked up. A rangy man in his fifties had sidled up to the table. He wore dark gray slacks and a beautiful gray cashmere sweater. This was Clarence "Big Boss" Dawkins. He was the Major League Baseball pitcher who had come back to the hood to run one of the city's biggest printing shops. Big Boss was a local legend. Everyone knew him. Kiki and Sherise had met him when he'd come to a yearbook club meeting.

"Well, well, if it isn't Big Boss Dawkins himself!" Tyson rose to shake his hand. "You planning to campaign for mayor in November?"

"Good to see you, Tyson," Big Boss chuckled. "You too, LaTreece. I'm not here to talk politics. I'm here to pay my respects to young Kiki. And to say congratulations for her being in the running for my scholarship."

"Thank you, sir," Kiki managed.

"You and the Ramirez girl are worthy candidates," Big Boss intoned. As he spoke, people at nearby tables shut up to listen. "No matter who wins, Kiki, I'm proud of your academic achievements. I hope after school you'll come right back to the hood to be the leader we know you will be."

Big Boss moved off. Geraldine brought the rest of the food, and they got down to the business of eating. Kiki, LaTreece, and Tyson dug in with gusto, but Sherise just pushed her eggs around on her plate. After the meal, she'd be catching the bus to the Eastside Mall where she worked at GG's clothing store. After many months in the stockroom, her boss was putting her on the sales floor.

"She should be excited 'bout that," Kiki thought. "Instead, she all mopey."

"You okay, sis?" Kiki asked with concern.

"Oh, I'm gravy," Sherise answered sarcastically. "Since it seem like there be only one daughter in this family. You."

LaTreece jumped in immediately.

"Now you listen here, Sherise Butler," LaTreece scolded. "There been plenty of times when you been all that, and nobody paid no never mind to your sister. When the yearbook got nominated for that big prize, everybody was all, 'Sherise! Sherise!' You need to turn down the green and turn up the love. You hear me?"

Sherise stared into her coffee instead of responding. Quick as lightning, Kiki saw her mother's hand flash across the table and lift Sherise's chin so that her eyes could laser into her daughter's face. "You *hear* me, young lady?"

"Mmm-hmm," was the best Sherise could muster. Then she pushed her chair back. "I'm goin' to work. Thank you for the meal. See you later."

Sherise headed for the exit. As she walked away, LaTreece's first instinct was to chase her, but Kiki saw her stepfather put a gentling hand on her arm.

"Let it go," he cautioned.

"Okay," LaTreece muttered. "But I ain't done wit' her."

"Let's all eat," Tyson suggested.

———

Kiki did try to enjoy her food. But after her sister's unhappy exit, Kiki found she didn't have much of an appetite.

"My name is Ki-ki Butler," Kiki said slowly so that the day-care kids could understand her.

"What she say?" a little girl in braids asked. Her name tag announced her as LaQuinta.

"Her name be Key-key Butler," another girl named Zenobia explained. Like LaQuinta, Zenobia couldn't have been older than four.

"That not a real name," LaQuinta scoffed.

"Is too," a young boy chimed in. Named Abernathy, he wore bright yellow shorts, a matching yellow shirt, and a name tag. His yellow shirt had Spaghetti-O sauce all over it from lunch. "Ki-ki. Like what a bird sing!"

"Hey!" A fourth boy pushed into the group. Called Skip, he was taller than the others. "I heard that! Her name not Key-key Butler. She named Ca-ca Butt-head! Ca-ca, like poop! Ca-ca!"

The kids fell over each other laughing. A chant started up. "Ca-ca! Ca-ca! Ca-ca!"

It was two hours since breakfast at the Fat Man. Kiki had arrived at the Towers day-care just after the kids had had lunch and was given the quickest tour by her new boss, Mrs. Phillips. The place was tucked behind the south building. It had a cruddy playground outside and an equally cruddy game room inside. There were also a couple of side rooms, a minuscule library, a kitchen and lunch-room, and a bathroom.

Since it was summer vacation, the day-care was jam-packed with kids. In fact, it was bedlam, with frazzled counselors chasing unruly kids everywhere.

Kiki had immediately spotted Nishell by the swings and waved to her. Nishell was so busy with a dozen little kids that she barely waved back.

Mrs. Phillips assigned Kiki to a group of four- and five-year-olds. Kiki thought she could interest them in a game of Duck-Duck-Goose.

She thought wrong.

"Ca-ca! Ca-ca! Ca-ca!" The chant had no end.

Kiki stood, helpless and embarrassed.

Mrs. Phillips rushed over. She was a giant of a woman—easily six foot three and two hundred pounds—in a blue dress.

"Hush!" she ordered.

The kids quieted.

Mrs. Phillips tilted her head at Kiki. "I want no more of ... of ... of that word from these children!"

"Yes, ma'am," Kiki said meekly.

Abernathy raised his hand slowly. In the presence of the boss, the kids had turned angelic.

"Yes, Abernathy?" Mrs. Phillips asked.

"I don't feel good."

Mrs. Phillips looked pointedly at Kiki. "Kiki will take you inside and let you rest on a folding cot. She will keep you company. Right, Kiki?"

Kiki was eager to please. "Definitely."

Abernathy swallowed. "I really don't feel good."

Mrs. Phillips's cell phone started to ring. "What are you waiting for?" she asked Kiki. "An invitation from the White House?"

"Oh. Sorry."

Angry at herself, Kiki picked up Abernathy. The boy draped his arms around her neck.

The boy retched. Again. Again.

Uh-oh.

"Argh! Blech!"

Kiki felt warm vomit spew all over her face and neck.

CHAPTER

4

Kiki swiped a wet paper towel at what used to be a Spaghetti-O that had just emerged from her left nostril.

For the last fifteen minutes, she'd been locked in the day-care bathroom, trying to wash off Abernathy's lunch. Fortunately, the day-care had a good shower and spare clothes. Kiki had showered thoroughly and then changed into a pair of gray cargo pants and a men's flannel shirt. Her own soiled clothes went into the trash.

"There is nothin' as nasty as a little kid barfin' on you," she thought sourly as she assessed herself in the mirror. "'Cept maybe for a little kid barfin' on you, and it goin' up your nose."

Okay. I be ready.

She took a deep breath and opened the bathroom door. A kid welcoming committee, led by Skip and Abernathy, was there to greet her. Nishell was supervising them.

"That be a miracle recovery," Kiki thought resentfully when she saw Abernathy grinning at her.

"You okay, girlfriend?" Nishell asked with concern.

Kiki nodded. "I think so."

"Ca-ca! Ca-ca!" Skip started.

"Drop it!" Nishell ordered.

Skip shut up.

"Mrs. Phillips wants you to watch these kids," Nishell told her.

"I can do that." Kiki knew that she'd gotten off to a rocky start at her new job.

She was anxious to prove herself—to Mrs. Phillips, the kids, and to herself.

"Cool. Then I got to get back to the playground. You comin' to Mio's tonight?" Nishell queried.

"Definitely," Kiki told her. "Sean too."

"Cool. I'll see you later, then. Good luck." Nishell took off, leaving Kiki with five little kids.

Kiki decided that Duck-Duck-Goose was still a good idea. "Come on, guys," she told them. "Let's try that game."

"No way we're playin' Duck-Duck-Goose!" Skip responded. "It's stupid."

"That game make me wanna barf!" a girl named Jess shouted.

"I already barfed!" Abernathy yelled.

Kiki felt control slipping away. "Come on. It's fun. Just try it."

"You play!" Skip told her. "I'm goin' to the swings with Nishell! She hot! You doodly-squat!"

The kids roared with laughter as Skip ran toward the door. Every single kid shouted "Yeah!" and followed him.

"Wait!" Kiki cried helplessly.

Two seconds later, they were gone. Kiki trudged after them. She knew if she couldn't get them to mind her, it was going to be a very long summer.

"Kiki, may I have a word?"

Kiki turned around. Mrs. Phillips stood unhappily at the far end of the corridor.

Uh-oh. Here it come.

Sure she was going to get reamed out, Kiki trudged back to Mrs. Phillips. "I'm sorry," she told her boss. "I'm tryin'."

"Kiki, I have a lot of experience," Mrs. Phillips responded. "I can see quickly who's going to succeed here and who won't. You're a bright girl. You're a nice girl. But we get extremely busy during the summer months, and I'm afraid you don't have the instincts to handle large groups of active children. This is, after all, your probationary period. I really think the best thing is for you is to find a summer position someplace else. I'm sorry."

Kiki couldn't believe it. "You're firing me on my first day?!"

Mrs. Phillips' voice was gentle but firm. "Let's just say you never started. That way, you don't have to say you've been fired."

"But I want to work here!" To be let go so quickly felt shameful. "I can do this! I just started!"

Mrs. Phillips shook her head. "If it was the middle of the year, I could train you. But not now. It's too crazy." As if to underscore Mrs. Phillips's point, a bunch of kids outside the door started wailing all at once. "You see what I mean."

Kiki's shoulders sagged. What was tough to digest was that Mrs. Phillips was making sense. The day-care was overwhelmed, and Kiki was not cutting it.

"Okay," Kiki murmured. "Thank you for the chance."

"Call me in the fall. Maybe I can fit you in then. Good luck. We'll mail your check."

There was nothing more to say.

For the third time in the last five minutes, Kiki trudged along the tiled corridor. This time, there'd be no return.

Kiki approached the front door of Mio's Pizza Palace on Twenty-Third Street, not far from Northeast Towers. After she left the day-care, she went home, changed again, and then trudged—that was definitely the word of the day—along Twenty-Third Street looking for a job.

It only took her a few hours to figure out that her goal shouldn't be a gig that might look good on a college application.

She should just find one with an actual paycheck.

She asked everywhere. Laundry—not hiring. Chicken joint—not hiring. Hardware store—not hiring. Auto supply shop—not hiring. Junk shop—not hiring. Medical clinic—not hiring.

Not hiring, not hiring, not hiring.

Mio's was her last hope for something local. If that didn't work, she'd have to spread out her search, but with the economy so bad, she wasn't optimistic.

Mio's was a prime hang for Kiki and her friends. It wasn't elegant. The tables were orange Formica and bolted to the floor, but they sold slices and drinks for a buck each on Friday and Saturday nights. The place was run by a white guy in his sixties with a head like a cue ball—Mio himself—who was a genius with dough, tomato sauce, mozzarella, and pepperoni.

Before she went in, her cell sounded with a text from Marnyke.

> Movies tmrw nite w me and Gabe?

She answered quickly.

> Let u know in morn

Marnyke texted right back.

Okay. Here we go.
She opened the door.

"Hey, Kiki!" Mio greeted her warmly. He wore a white apron and a white chef's hat. "What can I get you? Couple a slic-erinos? Dollar special don't start till six, but you're a good customer."

"No thanks, Mio," Kiki told him. "I don't want pizza."

"You feelin' okay, Kiki?" Mio asked, concerned.

"I'm fine."

Mio came out from behind the counter. "Then what? A calzone? Meatball sandwich?" He snapped his fingers. "Eggplant parm! That's what you need. I put two sandwiches on my mother's headstone whenever I go to the cemetery."

Kiki chuckled.

"You think I'm kiddin', kid? When I come back, they're gone. Someone's eatin' 'em. What's it gonna be?"

Kiki felt shy. "Well, I was wondering—do you maybe have a job opening?"

Mio shook his head sadly. "I'm sorry, Kiki. I wish I could help you. My grandfather—when he opened the place after the war—that's World War II—always had kids working here. Now, it's tough to make a go of it with just me. I would if I could."

"It's okay," Kiki tried to keep the disappointment out of her voice.

"Hey," Mio snapped his fingers. "Maybe when the economy—"

The door swung open.

Tyson walked in. "Hey, Mio, gimme two ..."

His voice trailed off as he noticed Kiki. "What are you doing here? Why aren't you at work?"

"They let me go," Kiki said with a sigh.

"They what?" Tyson was aghast.

"Let me go. Mrs. Phillips said I wasn't cuttin' it, an' she didn't have time to train me," Kiki explained.

"I know Sally Phillips. I'm going over there to give her a piece of my mind." Tyson turned back to Mio. "Make those two slices to go."

What do I even say? Where do I begin?

Kiki slid over to one of the Formica tables with orange plastic chairs and sat.

Tyson joined her while he waited for his slices.

"I got Mrs. Phillips that job," he told Kiki. "She owes me. She—"

"Tyson, stop!" Kiki's voice was sharp.

"What?"

"The little kids hated me. They called me Ca-ca."

Tyson shifted. "Really?"

Kiki nodded. There was a huge lump in her throat. She hadn't let herself feel the emotions of it all until now. "That was just to start," she said softly.

Mio brought over three slices of pizza and two drinks. "On the house, guys."

When Mio departed, Tyson lowered his voice. "Look, Kiki. I know a lot of folks in politics and whatnot. I know the mayor. You need a good job for your college apps. Let me make some calls for you."

It was a great offer, and Kiki knew she should take it. But after her failure at the day-care, she wanted to succeed on her own.

"No thanks, Tyson. I want to find my own job. That's why I'm in here. Course, there's no openings."

He looked at her with amazement. "You were ready to work at Mio's when you could be making calls for the mayor?"

"You got something against pizza?"

Tyson threw his head back and laughed. "I'm impressed. But you don't have to work here. Let me call the mayor for you."

Kiki looked right back at him, her eyes steely. "No."

She picked up a slice of pizza, folded up the edges, and—more as a statement than because she was hungry—took a serious chomp. As far as she was concerned, this conversation was done.

After her humiliation at the day-care, she'd find a job on her own. Or she'd die trying.

Kiki stood on the sidewalk outside Mio's, found Tia's number on her contact list, and pressed Send.

It was seven hours later. Some nights, Kiki and her friends went to Taco Bell. Sometimes they hung out by the cracked basketball court in the small park between the two Northeast Towers buildings. Most Friday and Saturday nights, though, they ended up at Mio's. Mio let them get as loud as they wanted. He even ran hip-hop through his sound system.

Kiki, Sherise, and Nishell—and their men—were there. Not Marnyke. She was hanging out with that white boy Gabe again. Tia wasn't a big hanger-outer, but Kiki had decided it might be cool to invite her.

"Who knows," she thought as the call went through. "Maybe she a different girl when school is out."

"Hello?" Tia answered.

"Yo, Tia. It's me, Kiki."

"Hi."

"So, I was wonderin', a bunch of us are hangin' at Mio's now. You wanna come down?"

Silence.

"I don't think so," Tia finally said.

"Come on, girl," Kiki urged. "Lighten up. School be over. Come out and celebrate with us."

"Can't," Tia told her. "I'm busy."

"Doin' what?" Kiki pressed.

"I'm busy, and that's all I got to say. Okay?" Tia responded.

"Okay." Kiki backed off. "Maybe another time."

"Maybe. See you."

Tia clicked off. Kiki was left with the phone at her ear.

Huh. That was weird. Wazzup wit' that girl?

Kiki went back inside to the table she was sharing with Jackson, Sean, and Nishell. Just as she got there, Mio called out that their order was ready.

"Nishell! Order up! Six slices, two Cokes, two Sprites, ten bucks!"

"I'm buyin' Kiki," Nishell told her.

"Her name not Kiki," Jackson cracked. "Her name be Ca-ca!"

"That not funny, man," Sean warned his cousin.

"Nah," Jackson kept going. "What be funny is that you wanna be wit' her!"

Kiki glared at Jackson and then stood with Nishell. "I'm comin' with you, Nishell. Yo' man suckin' the oxygen outta the room."

The two of them moved to the counter. "He gettin' on my nerves," Nishell groused as they waited for Mio to collect their money.

"What his problem?"

"I asked him," Nishell said. "He say 'nothin'.' He just out the pockets some-time."

"How he know 'bout the Ca-ca thing? You didn't tell him, did you?"

"You trippin'? My mouth shut. But he picked me up at work today and Skip was still Ca-ca-ing all over the place. Mrs. Phillips gave him a timeout, but that didn't do nothing."

Nishell hitched up her jeans over her serious tummy; she wore them with a pink T-shirt. Kiki, meanwhile, had on basketball kicks, gold shorts, and a men's white undershirt over a white bra.

She'd come to Mio's from the Northeast Towers basketball court where she'd been shooting around.

Kiki scowled. "If yo' man say it again, I'm gonna shove this pizza slice right down his fat trap."

"Why don't you and Sean hang wit' your sister?" Nishell motioned toward Sherise and Carlos, who were at a table near the door. Nishell looked embarrassed that her boyfriend was behaving so badly.

Kiki shook her head. "Sherise bein' a pain. My mom think she jealous of me."

"You happy or bummed she feel that way?"

Kiki pondered that for a moment. "Truth? Both."

"I hear you. Most of the time, all the attention on Sherise. Now she get to see what it feel like to be you." Nishell smiled, picked up the tray of food and drinks, and started back toward the guys.

If Kiki had hoped that a brief break would chill out Jackson, she was wrong. As she and Nishell approached, she saw Sean and Jackson were on their feet, ranking on each other. They were so in each other's grills that other kids had gathered around to watch the show.

"You got the ugly sister," Jackson ranted.

"Shut yo' big yap," Sean ordered, eyes blazing.

"Truth hurts, huh?"

Sean cocked his head to one side. "Why you bein' like this, Jackson? You forget to take yo' meds?"

The kids listening to the argument ooh'd and high-fived each other, which wound Jackson up more.

"Better'n my mama forgettin' to give me her nipple, like she done wit'chu!" Jackson fired back.

More oohs, aahs, and high-fives from the crowd.

"You bust on Kiki one mo' time," Sean warned, "I'm gonna bust your face."

That was enough for Kiki. She stepped between the two boys. "Jackson, give it a rest. Sean, let's get out of here."

"Ha!" Jackson hooted at Sean. "She got you by short hairs you ain't growed yet!"

Kiki could see that Sean was ready to slug his cousin. Not that Jackson didn't deserve it. But when the police came to break things up, she knew they'd take both guys in.

Maybe there's a way I can stop this.

"Tell you what," Kiki said to Jackson. "Bust on me all you want. Call me Ca-ca, even. But there's one thing you gotta do."

Jackson was suspicious. "What that? Kiss you? I wouldn't do that for all the chip in Vegas!"

"Shut yo' face, Jackson!" Sherise shouted.

Kiki looked at her sister gratefully. Sherise's support gave Kiki confidence for what she was about to say. "Let's take it to the basketball court. Me and Sean against you and anyone you want," Kiki challenged. "Two on two. Pick yo' teammate. If you win, call me anything you want. But if you lose, you gotta shut that damn pie hole for the rest of your sorry life. Is it a deal?"

Jackson seemed trapped. He'd just been challenged by a girl, but Kiki was no ordinary girl. She was great on the court, and everyone knew it. Sean was good too.

Kiki saw Sean nod.

"Bring it," he told Jackson.

Jackson shook his head. "Okay, cousin. Okay, Ca-ca. We takin' it to the court." He pointed at Carlos, one of the best players on the school team. "Carlos gonna be my teammate. Don't chu even think of sayin' no, Carlos. An' don't think of doggin' it!"

They'd play to fifteen by ones, half-court, on the cracked asphalt of the court at Northeast Towers, under the sketchy lights. Everyone from Mio's was lined up along one sideline, and a bunch of other people came over to watch too.

Folks loved a grudge match where there might be blood.

"Check!"

Kiki tossed the ball to Jackson, who flipped it back to her. The game was on.

Gotta get this going right. Watch this, Jackass.

Kiki dribbled twice and faked a drive to Jackson's right, who backed off a notch. That was all the separation she needed. She floated a jumper from sixteen feet.

Good.

"Ball!" she called as kids hooted at Jackson for his lousy defense

"Come on, smart girl," Jackson growled. "Try that again."

Kiki took the ball out again, fired a bounce pass to Sean, and then cut toward the hoop. Sean backed in on Carlos. Kiki ran to set a pick; Jackson followed. At the last moment, though, she cut to the far corner, where Sean lobbed a pass. A quick head fake gave her the room she needed to drive the baseline. Carlos moved to help defend her, so she zipped the ball to Sean, who hit the easy layup.

What a team! They were 2–0!

Carlos and Jackson switched on defense; Jackson took Sean, and Carlos guarded Kiki. It was a lot tougher for Kiki to score over Carlos's fierce defense. Back and forth the game went, with each side giving as good as it got. The crowd was into it. Some cheered for Kiki and Sean, some for Carlos and Jackson. Kiki heard her sister shouting for both teams.

The score knotted at 10. Then 12. Then at 13, as Sean rolled in a hook shot.

At 14–14, with Sean driving for the winning layup, Jackson fouled him hard in the back. Sean tumbled to the asphalt; everyone gasped.

He bounced quickly to his feet with two scraped knees. "What is yo' problem, Jackson?"

"You callin' foul?" Jackson taunted.

"Damn right I'm callin' foul!" Sean shot back.

"Then take the ball!" Jackson hurled the ball at Sean, who let it bounce off his hip and skitter away.

The tense crowd waited to see what Sean would do. If he threw a punch at Jackson, no one would blame him.

Once again, Kiki intervened.

She moved to Sean and put a hand on his shoulder. "I'm guarding Jackson."

"He an animal!" Sean shouted.

"He got nothin'," she said. "Take Carlos."

Off the foul, Kiki and Sean got the ball again. Kiki inbounded to Sean, who missed a wild shot from the corner. The rebound came far outside ... straight into Carlos's hands.

"Defense," Kiki thought. "They score, they win, an' I'm screwed."

Kiki hustled to guard Carlos, who lofted a perfect jumper from the right side. It headed for the bucket as the crowd moaned.

The ball rimmed the basket. Once. Twice. Then it rolled out and down ... and then rolled into Sean's hands.

Jackson cursed loudly.

"That ain't gonna help, Jackson," Kiki cracked as Sean whipped a pass back to her. She motioned Sean to clear the lane. He did. It was just Kiki and Jackson now.

"What my name?" Kiki demanded as she dribbled across the key.

Jackson said nothing.

"What my name, Jackson? What my name?"

Again, Jackson said nothing.

Kiki kept dribbling. "What my name, Jackson? My name be Winner!"

Four quick dribbles took her outside the three-point arc. She fired a turnaround shot that arched like a rainbow. It headed straight for the ten-foot-high pot of gold.

Yes!

Game over. The crowd went nuts. As Jackson stormed away with Nishell following him, Sean ran to Kiki and hugged her. Even Carlos offered props. "You the real deal, Kiki."

Sherise was right there too. "Way to shut Jackson's mouth."

"Thanks." Kiki wiped her brow with the back of her hand. "What was up wit' him?"

Sherise shrugged. "No clue. Maybe Nishell can find out something."

"If I were Nishell, I'd dump his ass," Kiki opined.

"Good game," Sean told her. "But maybe we can do something different tomorrow night."

Kiki nodded. This wasn't how she'd hoped the evening would end.

"For sure. Marnyke asked if we'd go to the movies with her and Gabe. I said I'd let her know."

Sean smiled even bigger. "Movie theaters are dark, right? Tell her yes."

Kiki went straight to the sideline, found her phone, and texted Marnyke.

Tmrw nite? Yes!

CHAPTER
6

"When our Lord Jesus Christ suffered on the cross," Reverend Mac declared, "Scripture says our Lord cried out!"

"Yes, He did!" someone in the church audience called.

"Yes, He did!" Reverend Mac responded. He was an imposing presence in his suit. "His words echo across the ages, right to our little church, don't they?"

"Preach it, sir!"

"Tell it to us!"

Kiki smiled. She loved that the preaching in black churches wasn't a one-way street. She never understood how white folks could just sit in their pews all still and silent, like rows of potted petunias.

Even so, there were plenty of Sunday mornings during the school year where church felt like another chore. Sundays in January, for example, when you could freeze your bones on the walk to the United African Methodist Church, which was six blocks east on Twenty-Third Street and then a half-block south on Davidson.

Even so, rain or shine, hot or cold, LaTreece would get everyone into their Sunday best. Tyson would be in a suit, LaTreece in a flowery outfit and fancy hat, and the girls in dresses too. They'd walk over as a family and settle into their favorite pew on the left side of the sanctuary. There were bigger congregations in the neighborhood, but the music here was wonderful. Best of all, Reverend Peter MacFarlane, whom everyone called Reverend Mac, kept services down to seventy minutes.

"After seventy minutes," he'd say, "even I go to sleep."

This Sunday, Kiki wore a long black dress; Sherise, who sat to her left, was in a flowered skirt and blouse combination. Tyson wore a suit and tie, while LaTreece had donned her choir robes. The UAMC tradition was for choir members to sit with their families until called on to sing. Kiki liked that. She liked to see her mom close her eyes and ride the waves of Reverend Mac's sermons.

"What did our Lord say to us from the cross?" Reverend Mac boomed. He wore a sky blue suit when he preached. "And how did He say it?"

"It's in Matthew," Kiki heard her mother whisper.

"He spoke in Aramaic, the common tongue of His time, to be heard by the common man," Reverend Mac explained. "He said—you can find this in your Bible in the book of Matthew—'Eli, Eli, lama sabachtani!' My God, my God, why hast Thou forsaken me? Why indeed? Because the Father was ready to bring his Son home!"

This was met with a chorus of encouraging shouts.

"Yessir!"

"Preach it, Reverend!"

"Bring us all home!"

"When we ourselves get called home," Reverend Mac asked, "how does He want us to be? What does He want us to bring? After all, we can't bring our cell phones and iWhatnots!"

The entire congregation rocked with laughter at this.

"My friends, the answer is found where all answers are found: in our Scripture. The apostle Paul says it in his letter to the Galatians—no, don't open your Bibles, listen to me!"

"Listen to the man!" LaTreece called.

Kiki met her stepfather's bemused eyes. Tyson wasn't nearly as religious as LaTreece. Sometimes Kiki thought he came to church just as a way to keep the family peace.

Maybe that's not such a bad reason.

Not that Kiki was having an easy time minding Reverend Mac herself. So much had happened these last couple of days. The scholarship announcement. The kissing with Sean at the river. The basketball last night. Tonight she'd be with Sean in a dark theater. Sean's warm lips—

Kiki felt her mom tug at her sleeve. "You're daydreaming."

"Sorry, Mama," she said reflexively, snapping her eyes back to Reverend Mac.

"What does Jesus want us to bring when we come home? Listen to Paul!"

The fruit of the Spirit is love,
    joy, peace, forbearance,
Kindness, goodness, faithfulness,
    gentleness and self-control ...
Since we live by the Spirit, let us
    keep in step with the Spirit!

As he sometimes did toward the end of a sermon, Reverend Mac strode down the center aisle to the center of the sanctuary. A hundred pairs of eyes followed his progress. Shouts of approval were everywhere now.

"To live by the Spirit is not to be rich," Reverend Mac thundered. "It is not to be clever, or smart, or sharp in business, or powerful, or to have folks 'fraid of you. 'The fruit of the Spirit is love, joy, peace, forbearance, kindness, and goodness!' Go forth in peace, be kind to one another, be good, and be filled with love! Amen! God bless you! God bless us all!"

The church organist started to play; the choir hustled forward and took its place on stage. A moment later, the church rocked with the sound of "Jesus Can Work It Out."

Kiki stood and sang every bit as loud as anyone.

She must have been praying for the right thing. When the service was over, and they'd said their good-byes, she hadn't taken more than five steps out the door when her cell sounded from a number she didn't recognize.

"Hello?" she answered cautiously.

"Hi, Kiki. It's Juanita Gutierrez, your sister's boss at GG's. Sherise tells me you're out of a job. Sorry 'bout that."

Kiki was impressed that Juanita even cared. "Thanks for callin'."

"Sherise starts work at one today," Juanita said. "Why don't you join her?"

CHAPTER

7

Kiki had just buttoned her GG's employee smock when Sherise came into the stock room. "You ready to get to it?"

Kiki nodded. "I owe you for this."

Sherise shook her head. She wore a white smock and white gloves. "You don't owe me nothin'. I'm the one who owes you an apology. Mom was right. I was all jealous of you. My head got up my you-know-where. I'm sorry."

Kiki was touched by her sister's words. It wasn't easy to admit that you were wrong. "It's nothin'."

"No, it's something, and I'm sorry. So don't thank me for helpin' you, little sister. If we don't help each other, who gonna help? Now listen up, I'ma tell you what to do."

It was two hours after church. They'd caught the bus together to the Eastside Mall where GG's was located. GG's sold clothes and accessories. Fifteen huge boxes of merchandise had come in late on Saturday, and it would be Kiki's job to prepare them for sale.

Sherise showed her the ropes. There were a dizzying number of things to do. Every item had to be unwrapped, tagged with its proper color, and put on its own special rack. There were eight tag colors. Blue for blouses, green for trousers, red for skirts, pink for undergarments, yellow for sweaters, and so on. "Got all that?" Sherise asked.

Kiki nodded hesitantly. "I think so."

Juanita's annoyed voice rang out on a loudspeaker. "Sherise Butler to the floor. Sherise Butler to the floor. Immediately!"

Sherise frowned. "Juanita's on the warpath. Gotta bounce. Good luck."

A moment later, Kiki was alone. The pile of boxes seemed to grow larger before her eyes. "Okay," she told herself. "Just take 'em one at a time."

Kiki started on the first box. It took forty-five minutes to unpack fifty blouses, tag them with green tags, and get them on the right rack. Then she moved to a box of trousers—red tags. That took another forty-five minutes. Then sweaters with pink tags. Forty-five more minutes.

It was tedious, dull, and lonely work. All that time, not a single person had come in or out of the—

"Hey, how you doin', Kiki? I was busy before."

Juanita, the store manager, stepped into the stockroom. Tiny Juanita wore a super tight black pullover and a white skirt, plus white gloves. The last time Kiki had seen her was at a party on the Northeast Towers roof. Then, Juanita's hair had been dyed bright red. Today, it was platinum blond.

"Okay, I think," Kiki told her.

"Let's see how you did." Juanita moved to the clothing rack that held the blouses. She took in her breath sharply. "Kiki! What do you think you're doing?"

"Excuse me?"

"This is all wrong! Blue tags for blouses not green tags!" Juanita stepped to the sweaters and moaned. "Yellow tags for sweaters. Not pink tags! Don't you listen?!"

Kiki's face burned. "I listen, yeah."

"Well, you listen like you got earplugs in. I'm gonna have to redo all this. You can't work in the stockroom. Go shadow your sister on the floor. Maybe you can sell clothes!"

"I'm sorry," Kiki said weakly.

"What are you standing there for?" Juanita shouted. "Go!"

Kiki went.

She spent the next three hours following Sherise around. She quickly saw that her sister had a gift for being kind, even to impossible customers.

For Kiki, though, three hours on the GG's floor felt like torture. By the time the store closed, Kiki knew she wasn't meant to work in the clothing business— not in the back room, nor on the sales floor. She'd rather have a stadium full of barfing day-care kids calling her "Ca-ca!"

"And this is the garage," Gabe said, almost apologetically, as they approached a long, low-slung, silvery structure. "My father spared no expense. Not that he ever does. Open!"

For the last thirty minutes, Gabe had been obviously embarrassed by his family's riches as he led Kiki, Marnyke, and Sean on a grand tour of his dad's estate in Majestic Oaks.

Embarrassed or not, the estate was breathtaking.

The ultra-modern mansion had twelve bedrooms and a movie screening room with fifty seats. Outdoors was a heated swimming pool, hot tub, grass tennis court, clay tennis court, paddle tennis court, and a basketball court. There was also an herb and vegetable garden that Gabe said was tended by a full-time gardener, plus a five-acre pond stocked with trout in case anyone wanted to catch their dinner.

There were also four guesthouses of two bedrooms each, one of which Gabe lived in. He said it was better than living in the main house with his dad, who spent most of his time on the computer managing his stock market portfolio and trading dollars against euros.

What this was all worth, Kiki had no idea. Tens of millions? Hundreds of millions?

More money than I'll ever see in my life, that's for sure.

The whole tour, Kiki noted how Marnyke clung to Gabe for dear life.

Gabe may not care about money, but Marnyke always knows which side of the bread has the sweet butter.

Kiki watched in shock as the massive garage door obeyed Gabe's voice command and silently lifted itself into the garage roof. She'd seen garages that held one or two cars. This one held a dozen. Not just any cars, either. She was no gearhead like Sean, but when the lights flicked on, she could pick out a tan Rolls-Royce, a yellow Lotus, a green-and-black Shelby Ford, a silver DeLorean with the gull-wing doors up, a red Ferrari, and a black car that looked like speed itself. It even had a spoiler on the back.

That's the one Sean ran to.

"Dude!" he shouted at Gabe. "You know what this be? This be a Maserati MC12 Corsa! Zero to sixty in three seconds! Two hundred miles an hour! You know what this baby cost?"

Gabe shrugged sheepishly. "My dad's into cars, what can I say?"

Sean circled the Maserati like it was the Kaaba in Mecca. "This be about a million an' a half big ones! Know how many of these they make a year? Twelve!"

It was fun for Kiki to see Sean so excited.

"You wish you had one, Sean?" she joshed.

"Hells yeah!" he answered.

Gabe shook his head and grinned slyly. "Can't help with that. But if you'd like to drive it …" He walked to the wall, opened a mahogany box, took out a set of keys, and tossed them to Sean. "Tank's full. Let's go."

"You're messin' wit' me, right?" Sean looked at the keys skeptically, his eyes round. "What your pops gonna say?" he asked warily.

"He'll never know," Gabe told him. "He doesn't drive 'em. Like everything else in life, he just likes to buy and sell 'em. If we still want to go to a movie, though, we gotta roll."

Sean's mouth spread into the biggest, widest grin Kiki had ever seen. "Let's roll. What about the girls?"

Gabe raised his eyebrows at Kiki and Marnyke. "Wanna take something out?"

"The Rolls!" Marnyke cried.

"The Rolls it is." Gabe found the keys and handed them to Kiki. "Let's meet back in, say, half an hour. Enjoy. Don't wreck it. That, he'd notice."

The guys headed out in the Maserati. The girls got into the 1965 Silver Cloud III. The front seats were plush white leather. The dashboard was custom wood. The instrument panels were circular. It smelled like money.

"Where you want to go?" Kiki asked Marnyke after the guys had pulled away.

"Nowhere," Marnyke confessed.

"Nowhere? You changin' your mind?"

"What if we crash?"

"Come on, 'fraidy cat. We gotta drive at least a little!" Kiki insisted, more excited than she'd thought about being behind the wheel of a Rolls-Royce. "I'll be careful."

With Kiki driving, they tooled around the estate a dozen times and then parked by the pond. It wasn't yet eight thirty; the sun was low in the western sky. The light through the pines was gorgeous. As the girls watched, a huge bird took off from one of the trees, circled the shoreline lazily, and then landed again.

"Whatzat?" Marnyke asked.

"Big Bird," Kiki said solemnly.

That cracked them both up.

"So, whatchu think of my new man?" Marnyke asked.

What do I think? I don't know. I don't really know him. But that's not what Marnyke wants to hear. I'm sure of that.

"He nice," Kiki told her.

"That ain't sayin' much. Guppies be nice, but they eat their babies. Gabe be special."

Okay. I gotta say what I gotta say. She may hate me, but she my bestie too.

"Marnyke, you my friend. I gotta be real wit'chu."

"You best be real wit' me," Marnyke answered.

Kiki took a big breath. "Okay. He white, and he rich. He actin' like money don't mean nothin' to him, but he still livin' here. You only know him a little, but you hangin' on him like you never want to let go. I bet you doin' the deed wit' him."

"You blame me?" Marnyke demanded. "He fine, an' he treat me real good. Why wouldn't a girl hit it wit' him?"

"Because he white and he rich!"

Marnyke folded her arms, and Kiki realized that had come out all wrong. She tried again.

"It's fine that he white, in theory," she said, choosing her words carefully. "I mean, Nishell got a white mom. And Nishell got rich grandparents too."

"But Nishell live in the same hood as us," Marnyke pointed out.

"That's my point," Kiki declared. "Marnyke, is this boy, Gabe, ever gonna come to our hood? If he do, how he gonna act? This be what he used to. *This!*"

She indicated the spectacular car, the fabulous estate.

Marnyke's voice got small. "I don't know. But chu know what, Kiki?"

"What?"

They were silent for a moment, as the huge bird—Kiki thought it might be a great blue heron—did another couple of circles before elegantly landing at the far end.

"What?" Kiki repeated.

"I don't know if Gabe gonna be my forever man," Marnyke admitted. She touched Kiki on the shoulder in a gesture of acceptance and friendship. "But if he ain't forever? He definitely good for right now."

CHAPTER
8

"Man, that was like flying!" Sean punched the air.

"Take it out it whenever you come," Gabe called. He was in the kitchen, getting beers and sodas. "Or any of the others. My dad doesn't care."

It was an hour later. The guys were back from their drive; the kids were all hanging out in Gabe's guesthouse at the north end of the estate. The place was all rough-hewn beams and wood-paneled walls and smelled faintly of fresh cedar. Not that it was rustic. There was a state-of-the-art kitchen, a living room with a fifty-five inch plasma TV and gorgeous furniture, two bedrooms, and a bathroom. Plus, Gabe had a huge collection of guitars; they stood in a row in racks against the wall.

Instead of going to the movies, they'd decided to watch one here or in the mansion screening room. Gabe told them he could download anything.

Sean was still all excited about the Maserati. It turned out that Gabe had directed him to a private track where the car could be opened up without fear of the cops. Sean had taken it to one hundred thirty miles an hour.

"Man, I'd do nothin' but drive those babies. 'Cept maybe soup 'em up. You wanna ride with me sometime, Kiki?"

"Kiki's dad drives a bomber," Marnyke quipped. "She ain't never been over fifty."

Kiki shook her head. "Nah, I don't think so. I like my life."

"I ain't gonna kill you," Sean assured her. "I know what I'm doin'."

"We'll see," Kiki dodged, wiping a little sweat from the soda bottle.

"I know what I want to see," Marnyke cooed to Gabe. He'd come back and nestled with her on the couch. Kiki and Sean were in two easy chairs. Gabe and Marnyke had beers; Kiki and Sean drank Cokes.

"What's that?" Gabe asked. He took a long swallow of the beer—some European brand named Stella Artois. Kiki was amazed that it was okay for Gabe to have beer in his place. Gabe had said his dad's only rule was that he didn't burn the place down.

Marnyke snuggled closer to him and batted her long eyelashes. "I was wonderin' if maybe we could put off that movie a bit so I can see yo' room."

Kiki and Sean shared a glance.

No doubt what Marnyke meant by "see."

"I supposed that could be arranged," Gabe said coyly.

"Perfect."

Marnyke stood and stretched sexily and then pointed at Kiki with a knowing smile. "We'll see you in an hour. Or maybe longer, dependin'. There's another bedroom, you know. Come on, Gabe."

She linked her arm through her man's, and they headed for the back bedroom.

"You know what they gonna be doin'," Sean said with a grin as the door closed.

"Yup."

Sean stood and stretched his sinewy arms like a cat. "I'm gonna go check out that other bedroom. How 'bout you come check it out wit' me?"

Without waiting for Kiki's answer, he walked toward the second bedroom.

"Sean, I—"

Sean stopped at the door and smiled at her. "Don't worry none. I always got protection. Got get yo'self ready. I'll be waiting. An' don't be nervous. We ain't never gonna get a better chance than this."

"But I'm a—"

Before she got to the word virgin, he stepped inside and closed the door.

Oh no.

Kiki was still a virgin. Not one of those virgins who swore she'd stay one till she got married, but definitely one of those virgins who wanted to want it more than anything when she decided to not be a virgin anymore.

Yet here she was. And there Sean was, behind the closed door of a bedroom in a guesthouse where there were no adults. She could hear laughter and sighs coming from Gabe's room. No doubt what they were doing.

She waited a minute. A minute more.

Go talk to him. Go in and tell him what I feel, how scared I am, how I'm not ready. Go.

She didn't go. She just stood as still as her heart between beats, while seconds ticked away.

Finally, she moved.

She didn't go to the bedroom. Instead, she left the guesthouse and followed a gravel path to the pond. There, she sat on a bench in the moonlight.

That was where Sean found her a half-hour later.

Sean pulled his Taurus to the curb in front of Northeast Towers. "You home."

"Thank you."

He killed the engine. "I'll walk you to the door."

His words were short. Clipped. Strained.

"You don't have to do that," Kiki assured him. "I'm fine."

He didn't respond. In fact, he'd barely said anything for forty-seven minutes since they'd departed the estate in Majestic Oaks.

Kiki tried to be polite. "I'm sorry the night didn't turn out like you wanted."

"You don' want me," Sean replied, his voice distant.

"That is not true!" Kiki answered hotly.

"That's not how I see it," Sean retorted. His face was dimly lit by a streetlight. "I'm a good man, Kiki. I don't drink. I don't smoke. I ain't a playa like my cousin Jackson, who I'm sure be hittin' it wit' Nishell when he ain't acting like a dumbass. I ain't no ghetto-boppa like yo' friend Marnyke—I hate to say that, maybe she changed, but that's how I always see'd her. I ain't a thug who gonna get you pregnant. I'm me. Sean King. An' I wan' you, baby. But you don' want me."

"I do want you!"

"You didn't tonight."

"I'm not ready." Kiki was almost tearful now.

"Who better to get ready with?" Sean asked.

"I don't know."

"Then lemme break it down for you," Sean told her. "What you ain't ready for be beautiful. It be the one thing that couples do that you don' do wit' just anyone. Maybe there be boys out there that don' wan' to hit it wit' you. You find yo'self one of those boys, 'kay? 'Cause I'm not one of them."

"Sean, that is not what I want and you know it!" Kiki shouted.

"Last time I looked, there be two people in this car. G'night, Kiki. Take care of yourself."

There was so much more that Kiki wanted to say, but she got out of the car and closed the door. She gazed at him through the open passenger window. He waited a brief moment and then pulled away.

That's when her tears actually came.

Kiki was still snuffling when she let herself into the seventh floor apartment and padded down the hallway to the bedroom that she shared with Sherise. She hoped her sister would be asleep; she was not up for a serious convo with no pickles and no onions.

No luck. The light shining through the crack under the door told her Sherise was still awake.

When she entered the room, Sherise was sitting on her bed near the open window playing a game on her cell phone. Since there was no air conditioning, a fan was running, and her sister was in a black bra and panties.

"I thought you weren't gonna be back till later," Sherise said without looking up from her cell.

Kiki couldn't manage a response. She just stood in the doorway, feeling rotten about what happened with her and Sean.

She saw her sister glance up, and her mouth fall open.

"Omigod!" Sherise was out of bed in a flash. "What happened? Are you okay? Kiki, you been crying!"

At the words "you been crying," Kiki started bawling all over again.

Sherise hustled her into the room and closed the door.

"Talk to me," her sister demanded. "Did anyone hurt you?"

Kiki shook her head and mumbled through her tears. "Nuh-uh. Only person who hurt me is me."

Sherise pursed her lips. "Whatchu mean? Here, take these."

She pressed some tissues into Kiki's hands and then helped Kiki to her own bed. Kiki sat on the scratchy blanket and tried to stop herself from crying. It took a long time, and Sherise kept an arm around her until there were no more tears to dry.

"Talk to me," Sherise urged.

"You promise you won't tell anyone?" Kiki looked at her sister through red-rimmed eyes.

"Lips sealed," Sherise assured. "Not unless someone hurt you. Then I'm gonna mess them up and mess up their family too."

Kiki talked. She told the whole story of the evening from her and Sean's arrival at Gabe's family estate in Majestic Oaks, right through that tortured exchange in Sean's Taurus.

"Did I do wrong?" Kiki pleaded. "Am I an idiot? Did I lose him forever?" She pointed a finger at Sherise. "What about you and Carlos? You two hittin' it?"

Sherise tilted her head slightly and nodded. "Mmm-mmm. I wouldn't say nothin' 'cause it ain't nobody's business but Carlos's and mine. But yeah, since you ask, we doin' it."

"You ever wish you wasn't?"

"Nope."

"Really?" Kiki pressed.

"Really. It's ... I don't know how to say this ... it's wonderful. I feel so close to him. It's not like Carlos's usin' me. Not at all. An' we careful too. I ain't walkin' around all pregnant and proud. I'm on the pill."

"Since when?" Kiki demanded.

"Hold it," Sherise cautioned. "We here to talk 'bout you and Sean. I'm just sayin' I'm careful, and no, Mama don't know, an' I ain't plannin' to tell her unless she ask me."

"When did you start?" Kiki asked.

Sherise shook her head intently again. "No! We talkin' 'bout you and Sean. So talk. You like Sean. He like you. How come you don't want him to be your first?"

"That the problem!" Kiki raised her voice so loud that her sister shushed her. "I don't got a good reason. I got the right guy, I got the right time, I got the right place. I got everything a girl would want, 'cept the wantin' to do it."

Sherise went to get a glass of water that was on her nightstand. She handed it to Kiki, who drank gratefully.

"So, whatchu sayin' is," Sherise summarized, "you don't want to 'cause you don't want to."

"Somethin' like that," Kiki agreed, realizing how lame-ass that sounded.

"That sounds okay to me."

Kiki gazed up at her sister in disbelief. "Really?"

"Really," Sherise assured her. "People doin' it and not doin' it for all kinda reasons. Nishell was hittin' it with Jackson, but now she not hittin' it because Jackson flunked the whole year. He not happy. You saw that."

"How you know that's why Jackson's being such a tool?" Kiki challenged.

Sherise sighed. "Nishell called me tonight. She got a mind of her own. You got a mind of your own. But you gotta understand that Sean's allowed to have a mind of his own too."

"My not hittin' it with Sean is not a good reason for him to dump me!" Kiki responded angrily. "Doin' it ain't that big a deal."

Sherise folded her arms. "If it ain't that big a deal, then how come you don't want to do it with him?"

Kiki felt herself getting mad. She'd confided in her sister, and this is what she got in return? Getting sassed and made fun of? She stretched out on her bed and put her hands under her head, expecting to get angrier and angrier.

The opposite happened.

The longer she lay there, the more she realized her sister had asked a great question.

"If it ain't that big a deal, then how come you don't want to do it with him?"

She answered the question in her head.

I ain't doin' it because I ain't ready to do it. That's a big deal to me. Sean has to live with that, and I gotta live with that. Even if it mean we can't be together.

"Thanks, Sherise," Kiki said suddenly.

"What for?" Sherise asked.

Kiki smiled for the first time in a long time. "For bein' real. And for bein' you."

What is that?" Kiki pointed to a transformed corner of the family living room.

Sherise turned her palms up and shook her head. "No clue."

It was Monday morning. The two sisters had slept late. Sherise didn't have to be at the store until noon. As for Kiki, while she knew she could go back to GG's, she also knew it would be best if she could find another job. That would be her project for the morning. She'd already left Juanita a voicemail saying so.

Now they were on their way to the kitchen for morning coffee. But an overnight change in the living room stopped them dead in their tracks.

"Surprise!"

Tyson and LaTreece suddenly appeared in the opposite entrance to the living room. They were dressed for work. As for the living room corner—until last night it had been empty—now, there was a brown desk, black office chair, booted-up laptop computer, SAT and achievement test prep books, notebooks, a container of pens and pencils, and even what looked like a couple of college application forms.

Above it all was a banner that read:

KIKI'S KOLLEGE KORNER

"What do you think?" Tyson chortled.

"We want you inspired," LaTreece beamed at Kiki. "Now you got everything you need to make somethin' of your life! You our super-duper college girl!"

For a brief instant, Kiki was flattered. Then she noticed Sherise's stony face, and the way her sister's petite body seemed to be caving in on itself inside her ratty plaid bathrobe.

Kiki instantly understood why Sherise was so upset. It turned her happiness to icy fury.

"What do *I* think?" Kiki repeated Tyson's question. "What do I think? I hate it. No. I more than hate it."

"*What?*" Tyson was shocked. LaTreece looked gut-punched.

Kiki marched over to her mother and stepfather. "I think you forgettin' that there's two kids in this family."

"We know that!" LaTreece said defensively. "We just wanted—"

"If you know it," Kiki accused, "you don't act like it. Just because I got better grades than my sister don't make me no better than her. It don't mean she won't make somethin' out of her life too. Sherise be as good as me. Maybe better."

"Kiki, you're taking this the wrong way," Tyson told her.

"No. You ain't bein' fair," Kiki corrected. "You set up this corner for me with a computer and everything. What about Sherise? What you doin' for her? She can go to college too. She ain't flunkin' out like Jackson Beauford. An' if she don't go to college, so what? She'll do fine anyway!"

"We love both of you!" LaTreece proclaimed. "Don't you girls know that?"

Kiki took a moment to glance at her sister again. She saw respect in her sister's eyes, but also simmering anger at LaTreece and Tyson.

"Here's what I know," Kiki said, turning back to her parents. "I know what Reverend Mac said at church. He said Jesus didn't talk about taking the SATs or Spellman or Harvard. If he did, maybe you wasn't listenin' as well as you think you was."

She knew she was dangerously close to the line of acceptable family behavior, but she didn't care. Sherise had been there for her last night, straight up. She was going to be there for Sherise this morning.

For a moment, the living room was as silent as a cemetery.

Then LaTreece stepped to the corner, took down the "Kiki's Kollege Korner" sign, and tossed it in the trash. Silently, Tyson joined her. They boxed up the study books. In fact, as the girls watched, they didn't stop working until there was nothing left in the corner but an empty desk and chair.

Finally, parents faced kids.

"Girls, I apologize to both of you. Especially you, Sherise," LaTreece confessed.

"I do too." Tyson's eyes flicked from Kiki to Sherise and back again. "It's easy to forget what really matters. If you want this stuff, take it to your room. It's yours. I mean, for both of you."

Kiki turned around to look at Sherise, who still stood near the entrance to the living room. Her eyes asked an unspoken question: was their parents' apology enough?

Sherise nodded slowly and came to join Kiki.

"Okay. Apology accepted," Sherise said softly.

"I agree," Kiki told LaTreece and Tyson.

Silence reigned for another moment.

Then LaTreece gazed up at Tyson. "You need to listen harder in church, Tyson."

Tyson fake-bristled. "Don't seem to have helped you none!"

Everyone laughed. LaTreece held her arms out for a group hug. The girls went to her.

"Thanks," Sherise murmured to Kiki as they moved into their mom's loving arms.

"You're welcome, sis," Kiki told her as Tyson enveloped all of them.

Wrapped in the arms and warmth of the family she loved, Kiki got an idea. She'd done one important thing this morning. Maybe there was another she could do.

CHAPTER

11

Forty-five minutes later, Kiki entered the day-care playground dressed in basketball shorts and a T-shirt, with her braids back in a ponytail. Just as it had been the day she was let go, the day-care playground was madness, with kids running everywhere and frazzled counselors trying to control them.

She spotted Skip holding court over by the merry-go-round. Skip saw her too.

"Hey, hey!" Skip shouted. He pointed and jumped around like he'd just won a candy lottery. "Ca-ca be back! Ca-ca! Ca-ca!"

The other kids nearby took up the chant. "Ca-ca! Ca-ca! Ca-ca!"

Kiki marched over to them and dropped to one knee. "Stop that! Stop that right now!"

Maybe it was the no-nonsense tone of her voice. Or maybe it was a miracle. Whatever the reason, the chant stopped.

"Gather 'round me!" Kiki ordered.

The shocked kids—including Skip—meekly circled her.

"If I ever, ever hear those words again," Kiki warned, "you will deal with Mrs. Phillips. You will deal with your mamas or your daddies. An' when you done dealin' with them, you gonna deal with me!"

She glared at Skip, the ringleader. "Am I understood, Skip?"

The boy nodded humbly.

"Say 'Yes, Kiki, I understand,' " Kiki ordered, eyes blazing.

"Yes, Kiki," Skip muttered and kicked a little at the dirt. "I understand."

"Nicely done, Kiki."

Kiki looked up. Mrs. Phillips was now standing behind her, arms folded. "What I want to know, Kiki," Mrs. Phillips asked, "is what happened between Saturday and now?"

"Dunno." Kiki was honest.

"If I'd known you had that in you, you'd still have a job. But I've hired someone else. She starts in an hour. What brings you to us today?" She looked at the children. "Run on and play!"

The kids scattered, leaving Kiki alone with the day-care director.

"I know I can't work here anymore," Kiki told her. "And I don't blame you for letting me go. But I was wondering ... maybe I can volunteer? I'm real good at basketball and school. There's gotta be a way I can help."

"You want to volunteer."

Kiki nodded. Mrs. Phillips glanced skyward, as if seeking divine guidance. Then she gazed at Kiki again. "I believe there is something you might be able to do. At least you can try. Follow me."

Ten minutes later, Kiki was alone in the day-care library—a windowless room with five bookshelves of kids' books, several tables and chairs, and a couple of whiteboards. Shortly afterward, Mrs. Phillips returned, hand-in-hand with a small girl in the Northeast Towers yellow day-care T-shirt. She had braids and scuffed sneakers, kind of like a mini-Kiki.

"This is Geneva. She just finished first grade but barely reads," Mrs. Phillips confided to Kiki. "I think she just needs the right teacher. Want to give it a try?"

"Maybe she just needs the right book," Kiki suggested. "Hi, Geneva. I'm Kiki."

"Hi, Kiki. I'm a bad reader."

"Let me decide if that's true," Kiki told her as Mrs. Phillips slipped discreetly out of the room.

Now Kiki was alone with the girl. She'd never actually helped a kid with their reading before.

Where to start?

There was a small whiteboard leaning against one of the bookcases. Kiki got it and found a black marker.

"What we doin'?" Geneva asked as Kiki erased the whiteboard.

"What's your favorite word?" Kiki asked. She wondered if what she'd said before was true. That it wasn't that Geneva was a bad reader; it was more that she hadn't found the right book.

The right story always has someone you can relate to.

Let me give her a story she can relate to.

"That's a weird question! You're weird!" Geneva laughed.

"Yep, I'm weird," Kiki admitted. "The weirdest. But my favorite word is my own name."

She wrote KIKI in all caps at one side of the whiteboard. "Now, how about you? What's your favorite?"

"Okay. My favorite word is Geneva," the girl declared.

Kiki feigned confusion. "How you spell that?

"G-E-N-E-V-A."

Kiki scrawled those letters on the whiteboard. "And what is Geneva's favorite food?"

Geneva answered immediately. "Pizza!"

"P-I-Z-Z-A." Kiki wrote that near Geneva's name. "What does that spell?"

"P-I-Z-Z-A spells pizza!" Geneva announced.

"I think we should write a story about you and pizza," Kiki decided. "Then we can read it together."

The girl was awestruck at the idea. "We can do that?"

Kiki wiped the whiteboard clean. "Not only can we do that, we gonna do that right now. What should the first sentence be? Keep it easy 'cause I'm not a very good reader either," she fibbed.

"Okay. How about, 'There was a girl named Geneva who loved pizza,' " Geneva suggested.

"That's perfect!" Kiki wrote those words in big letters on the whiteboard. "And how about this as the second sentence: 'There was not a single kind of pizza that Geneva would not eat.' "

"That's not true!" the girl cried. "I don't eat pizza with flies."

"Okay," Kiki smiled. "Make that a sentence," she urged.

"Okay. 'The only pizza Geneva did not eat was pizza with dead flies.' "

"Wonderful!" Kiki wrote that sentence on the whiteboard too.

Back and forth they went. The first paragraph of the Geneva pizza story grew to six sentences. Kiki made sure to keep it easy. Finally, it was done.

"Ready to try it out?" Kiki asked.

Geneva nodded gravely. Then she read slowly from the whiteboard.

"There was a girl named Geneva who loved pizza. The only pizza that Geneva did not eat was pizza with dead flies. Flies are not good on pizza. It did not matter if the rest of the pizza was the best pizza ever. If there were dead flies in the topping, she would send the pizza back to the chef. He could eat it!"

Geneva nailed it.

Kiki felt fantastic. Then she heard clapping from the doorway when she was done. She looked up. There stood Mrs. Phillips, flanked by two people. One was obviously Geneva's mother, because Geneva cried "Mama!" and flew to her. Mother embraced daughter.

"I can read!" Geneva announced proudly.

"I heard you!" said her mother. She was very young.

Mrs. Phillips announced the other person as the new day-care student worker. But she needed no introduction. Kiki knew her well. Maybe too well.

It was Tia, dressed in new jeans and a new white T-shirt.

"Hey, Tia," Kiki called. "Welcome to the day-care."

"Hey," Tia said politely.

"Tia said she knows you from school," Mrs. Phillips reported. "Tia, let's continue your tour. Kiki, stay there. Geneva's mom wants to talk to you."

When Tia and Mrs. Phillips had departed, Geneva's mom came over to Kiki with her happy daughter in her arms. The young mother looked like a teenager herself in ripped jeans, a thin tank top, and visible red bra straps.

She ain't much older than me. If I ever get pregnant as young as she did, let me eat pizza with dead flies for the rest of my life.

"I'm Paris." The woman introduced herself. "I never—I didn't know she could read like that!"

"Maybe she didn't know, either," Kiki responded.

"Whatever you doin', keep doin' it. I was never good at school. I want Geneva to do good." Her pretty face was serious. "I could pay you ten dollars an hour if you'll tutor ·her. I don't got time, and Geneva's got no daddy. Maybe every day, two hours. I know some other moms in the hood who would do the same. You'll have more kids than you can handle!"

Kiki was floored. This woman was ready to hire her as a tutor for her daughter on the basis of six sentences. She was flattered, but also wary. This Paris was a single mom. Where was she going to get twenty dollars a day?

"That a lot of money," Kiki commented.

"I'm a dancer," the woman said with pride. "I got plenty of cash."

Kiki knew what that meant. *Omigod. This little girl has a stripper for a mother!*

Then Kiki thought again.

Teaching kids to read? That's the perfect thing to do for the summer. It's fun. It'll make money, and it'll look good on a college application. Most of all, I'll do good. So what if her mom be workin' as a stripper? She puttin' her daughter first.

But what if I get too busy? Hey! I know ...

It had been a morning of ideas. Kiki had just gotten another one.

"I'd love that," Kiki told Paris. "Is it okay if someone helps me out?"

I need to ask you something," Kiki told Tia, who was in the kitchen making peanut butter sandwiches. "But I need to know that you're okay."

"Of course I'm okay. Why wouldn't I be okay?"

" 'Cause you acting strange, all week. I mean, you strange all the time, but you stranger than strange now." Kiki grinned, trying to turn her observation into a joke.

Tia didn't find it funny.

"I'm fine," she repeated. "If you're saying this because I didn't want to come to Mio's the other night, I was studying."

"What for? School's out."

"SATs," Tia said flatly. She kept spreading peanut butter. "Anything else?"

Kiki shifted her weight uncomfortably. Tia was already getting ready for the college exams? Wow. Plus, the girl was sending out a big chill.

Still, there was something she wanted to ask. "Well, here's the thing."

"Yes?" Tia asked diffidently.

Do I really want to say this?

I do.

"Here's the thing," Kiki told her. "I've got a chance to tutor a girl. To get her to read better. If her mom is right, there'll be more kids. I was thinking that maybe we could do a tutoring business together. I'll bet we'll get a lot of kids. I know you're working here, but on weekends and stuff, it'd be perfect. And colleges will love it."

"Ri-ight." Tia made another sandwich.

It wasn't an enthusiastic response, but Kiki plunged on. "And I was thinking ... if we team up on that, maybe we should team up on the scholarship too."

Tia finally looked up. "What do you mean?"

"I mean, study together. Do community service together. Be valedictorians together. We be the best students at the school, but I been in this hood a lot longer than you. It ain't an easy place to be a student. People gonna knock you down jus' cause they can. I'm sayin' we'll do better if we do it together—"

"And split the scholarship, you mean," Tia went on.

"That's exactly what I mean," Kiki said happily.

Tia slammed her hand down on the table so hard it made Kiki jump.

"No!" She stood to face Kiki. "No way!"

Kiki was stunned. It had seemed like such a good idea, in every sense of that word.

"But ... but why not?"

"You and I are competing, Kiki," Tia's voice was ice cold. "I want something. You want that same something. You are willing to take half of it. I am not. I don't want to share it. I want to win it. If I win it, you are a loser. I don't want to be friends with a loser."

"Loser? That's a hell of an attitude," Kiki said as fury riled her stomach at the bee-yotch Tia was being. "I tutored you when your English wasn't this good. You should be thankin' me."

"I thanked you then, thank you very much. I need the scholarship more than you do," Tia maintained. "Which is why I'm going to win, and you're going to lose."

Kiki fumed. Tia had thrown her good-ness back in her face.

"No," she told Tia. "I'm goin' to win. When I do, remember this convo. If you don't remember, I'll remind you. Good-bye, Tia."

Five minutes later, still angry about Tia but determined to beat her, Kiki left the day-care and turned toward the entrance to Northeast Towers. She wanted to change and then go talk to Tyson about using the Towers commu-nity room for her tutoring business. She'd just reached the spot where she'd gotten out of Sean's Taurus after their horrible ending the night before when she heard her name called loud.

"Hey, smart girl!"

She looked up the sidewalk toward Twenty-Third Street. Sean was trotting toward her, dressed in blue mechanic's coveralls. He'd obviously come from work at the garage.

He looked fine. Real fine.

What does he want?

"Hey, mechanic," she said simply.

"I been missin' you," he told her.

She felt a lump grow in her throat at these words. "I miss you too."

"I've been doin' some thinking about our last convo," he admitted. "How 'bout you?"

She had been thinking too. But she wasn't ready to hit it with him. No matter how fine he looked.

"Me too," she said softly.

"Lemme tell you what I been thinkin'," he offered. "I been thinkin' I miss you too much to be wit' anyone else. I been thinkin' you make me happier than anyone else. I been thinkin' that if you ain't ready to be doin' it, I'm ready to wait. Long as we don't have to wait till the next century."

Did he just say it's okay if we don't start doin' it? I think that's what he sayin'. I know that's what he's sayin'!

"Oh, Sean ..." She was overwhelmed.

He stepped toward her. "Then we good?"

She couldn't even form the word *yes*. She just nodded.

He opened his arms. She moved into them; they embraced and kissed right there on the sidewalk with people streaming by on both sides of them.

The words of Christopher Okigbo came roaring back to her.

I have fed out of the drum
I have drunk out of the cymbal
I have entered your bridal chamber;
    and lo,

I am the sole witness to my
   homecoming!

The kiss didn't take Kiki to the next
century, or even to next year's homecoming.

It just felt like it did.